In my heart,
I am a dancer

នៅក្នុងជំរៅចិត្ត, ខ្ញុំជាអ្នករាំ

Philadelphia

FOLKLORE
PROJECT

A program of the Asian Folk Arts Education Project
A collaboration between the Philadelphia Folklore Project and
the Office of Curriculum Support, School District of Philadelphia

Project coordinator: Teresa Jaynes
Book collective: Teresa Jaynes, Debora Kodish, René J. Marquez and Deborah Wei
Design: Ife Designs and Associates
Printing: Worzalla Publishing

ISBN: 0-9644937-2-1

Published by the Philadelphia Folklore Project
1304 Wharton Street
Philadelphia, PA 19147
215-468-7871

© 1996

This project was undertaken with the support of the National
Endowment for the Arts—Folk Arts Program, the Samuel Fels Fund,
and the Pennsylvania Council on the Arts.

Photo credits: All photos courtesy of the Philadelphia Folklore Project.
Cover photo: Jane Levine. **p. 2-3.** Background photo: Angkor Wat, courtesy of Denis Horgan. **p. 6.** Vanna Sieng and Chamroeun Yin (age 26) Tep Manoram dance, Chunbury refugee camp, Thailand, 1980. Courtesy Chamroeun Yin. **p. 7.** Backstage at the Kennedy Center, Washington, D.C. before a performance, c. 1982. Courtesy Chamroeun Yin. **p. 13.** Chamroeun's sister Sunnary Yin, standing, and mother, Van Sék, sitting, in Cambodia, c. 1981-2. Courtesy Chamroeun Yin. **p. 18.** Tom Kramer and Chamroeun Yin, 1988. Courtesy Chamroeun Yin. **p. 19.** Tom and Chamroeun's brother, Kim Sour Yin, and his nephew and niece, c. 1994. Courtesy Chamroeun Yin. **p. 20.** Chamroeun Yin puts on a headpiece before a dance performance. Photo: Thomas B. Morton. **p. 23.** Ramaso mask, demon of the storms, made by Chamroeun. **p. 25.** Chamroeun's masks, l-r: Mask of the demon's servant, Ramaso, Ravana (10-faced demon). **p. 26.** Chamroeun teaching a student, c. 1987. Photo: Thomas B. Morton. **p. 28-9.** The Cambodian Classical Dance Group, c. 1981-2. Chamroeun is fifth from the left. Courtesy Chamroeun Yin. **p. 29** inset: Chamroeun's teacher Peou Khatna, bottom right, and other dancers. Courtesy Chamroeun Yin. **p. 30, 32**, photos: Jane Levine.

In my heart, I am a dancer

នៅក្នុងជំរៅចិត្ត, ខ្ញុំជាអ្នករាំ

By Chamroeun Yin

Photographs by René J. Marquez
Additional photographs by Jane Levine and Thomas B. Morton

Edited by Deborah Wei and Debora Kodish
Khmer translation by Chiny Ky

Philadelphia Folklore Project

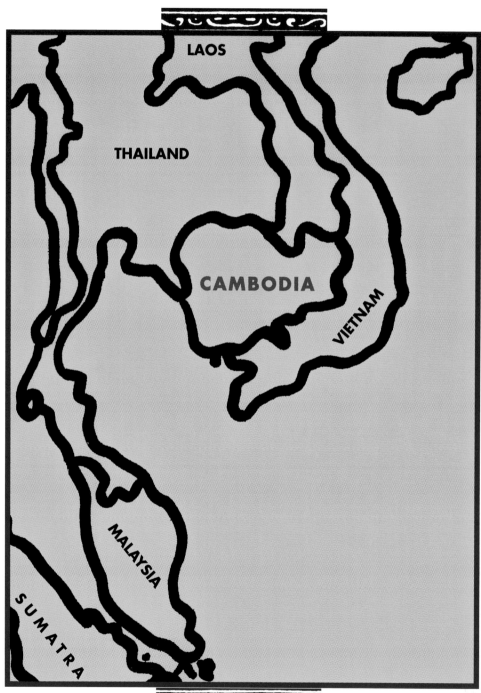

About this book

This book is the result of an evolving process in which we are trying to develop a "critical" approach to folk arts. In our work in Philadelphia, we have seen many teachers turn to folk arts to bring multicultural education into their classrooms. While this is gratifying, teachers often lack resources which can deepen and complicate their understanding of these traditions. We don't want folk arts to be a "quick fix." We know that folk arts are not always safe, beautiful, and non-controversial

Folk arts, as used every day in peoples' lives, are very complex. Asians and Asian Americans practicing folk arts here in the United States are layering these traditions with new contexts, new meanings. A decision to maintain culture and to practice traditional art is not necessarily safe for an artist. It can require sacrifice and a fight for cultural survival and respect in the face of many obstacles. It is a choice that must be continually made over and over again.

And so our challenge, as educators and folklorists (and as parents), is to help others look more closely at folk arts. How can we raise critical questions which address some of the harder issues of race, class and gender which are often at the center of how folk arts are practiced and received in the U.S.? Is it possible to do this at all grade levels? And if we believe it is possible and important for young children to face some of these issues, how do we help them do it? These were the questions which we sought to address, and on which we are continuing to work.

We feel that to responsibly educate, we need to present a full picture to our students. Non-critical folk arts in some ways may be as bad as no folk arts at all. Silence and failure to acknowledge some of the harder issues can lead to superficial understandings, and may actually reinforce stereotypes rather than challenge them. What happens if students see Chamroeun's dance only as something beautiful? To some degree, they may learn to recognize the beauty, grace and artistry of the dance. But they may also walk away from the experience more firmly entrenched in a vision of Cambodian dance as foreign, exotic, or mysterious—and as something removed from them. How much they would miss by not knowing of the struggle which Chamroeun faces to maintain his art, or of the many sides of this man, or that they may have seen him, one day, buying fabric in a mall. These ideas are the ones which bring students to new levels of understanding.

This book is one piece of a long, collaborative, and continuing process in which we are engaged. Other books and media projects, documentation of our own work, and teachers' guides are also in process. For additional information about this and other initiatives, please contact us: Philadelphia Folklore Project, 1304 Wharton St., Philadelphia, PA 19147, (215) 468-7871.

5

Acknowledgments

We are grateful to children at Samuel Powel Elementary School: Cally Adamson-Jackes, James Allie, Thomas Brown, Violette Carb, Tyran Davis, Hadiya Deloatch, Allison DeMarco, Brian Franklin, Ashley Hayward, Brandon Henson, Ashley Hooks, Kyree Hyman, Lilly Kay, Ruth Kodish-Eskind, Sarah Kodish-Eskind, Danielle Lewis, Milton Lindsay, Andrew Lyn, Malik Mack, Michael McHugh, Ashley Perkins, Joelle Phillips, Maham Rizvi, Brittany Rogers, Derek Rouse, Meg Taylor, Kristina Thurin, Voothy Vongvone, Nateshia Wanamaker, and Qian Yang. Thanks also to Angela Valez and her third grade class, P.S.13, Clifton, N.J.

Many thanks as well to educators: Penny Barchfield-Venet, Sabra Cameron, Elaine Culbertson, Donna Erikson, Eileen Feldgus, Helen Gym, Rhoda Kanevsky, Chiny Ky, Judy Lewis, Deborah Menkart, Elizabeth Nordell, Barbara Pressman, Ruth Tatum, Hue Tran, and Katie Zimring.

I am a dancer.

My name is Chamroeun Yin. At home, people would call me Roeun, for a nickname. (You can call me "Ran.") I was born forty years ago in a country called Kampuchea. The English name for my country is "Cambodia."

Ever since I can remember, I always had a feeling in my heart for dance. My father was a musician. When I was a boy, he would play music. When nobody could see, I would dance. I danced secretly because I was embarrassed. I didn't really know how to dance, and I made up my own steps. I was afraid that it would look crazy to other people. But I loved to dance, very, very much.

Then one time, a very good court dancer came to our school. Court dance is a special kind of dance that once was done only in the palace of the Cambodian king. When I saw it, my heart went to this dance. I thought it was very beautiful. But when I was a boy, I didn't have a chance to learn. The people who knew how to do court dance lived far away in the capital city of Cambodia where the king had his palace. I never thought it would be something I could do.

ខ្ញុំជាអ្នករាំ

When I was a boy, there was a long war in my country. In 1975, when I was 21 years old, there was a new, very cruel government in Cambodia. My whole family, and many other people, became refugees. Because of the war, we had to run away from our homes and try to escape to safety in another country. My mother, my sister, my brother and I were separated during this time. It was very terrible and many people died.

When I could, I escaped. A friend and I crossed through the jungles and the mountains to a refugee camp in Thailand, where other people had also come to be safe. In this camp, I began to study dance, learning from court dancers who were also refugees. They taught dance to help people be happy again and to remind us of our country.

I am a tailor.

I first learned to sew in Cambodia before the war. I learned from my aunt and my second cousin. They were very good at making clothes. They let me work with them and learn. I didn't get paid while I was learning. Making money was never something I wanted. I just wanted a chance to learn to sew because I liked being able to make clothes that looked just the way I wanted.

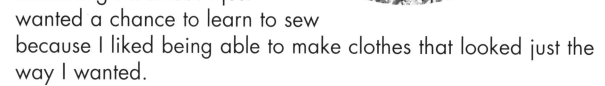

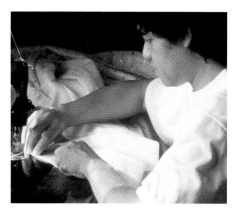

When I escaped from Cambodia, it was a very dangerous and hard journey, but I brought my sewing machine with me, carrying it on the back of my bicycle. I also brought my notebook which had all of my drawings about how to make different kinds of clothes. I carried these things through the jungles in Cambodia, and across the mountains into Thailand. I thought that this was how I could make a living if I survived. I also brought my scissors, tape measure and

ខ្ញុំជាអ្នកកាត់ដេរ

tracing paper. I had some jewelry from my mother and one set of clothes to wear. I carried all of this in a bag on my back. It took me about three days to make the journey to Thailand. I walked

and ran the whole way. There were exploding land mines, and robbers. It was very dangerous and I was very frightened.

I stayed in the refugee camp in Thailand for a little more than one year. When I was 26 years old, I was allowed to come to

resettle in America. I had to leave my sewing machine behind when I came here. They wouldn't let me carry it on the airplane.

When I came to America, I bought myself another sewing machine just like the old one. It doesn't use electricity. I make it work by moving my feet up and down on a special kind of pedal, called a treadle. I like my sewing machine. It is easy to use and it also reminds me of my life in Cambodia. Using my legs to peddle is good exercise, too!

I am a son and a brother.

I haven't seen my mother and sister for almost twenty years—since 1979. Because of the war back then, many families were separated, just like mine was. Many, many people died. It was very hard to know who was safe and where people were. There were no phones or mail or anything like that. I always feel sad when I think about that time.

My mother and sister are still in Cambodia. We used to live near the city, but our house was destroyed during the war. Now, instead of a house, you can only see land and grass. So they both moved to a different house, farther from the city. Cambodia is a very poor country. It is still hard for people to have enough to eat. I sometimes send my mother and sister some of the money I earn from my work. I miss them very much and they miss me, too.

I worry about my mother and sister. I would like to go to visit them sometime, but there is still fighting in my country. It is still very dangerous. If peace comes to Cambodia, I will try to go to see them.

ខ្ញុំជាក្មួននិងជាបងប្រុសម្នាក់

13

I am a gardener.

To tell the truth, when I first came to America in 1981, I missed some of the food that I used to be able to eat in Cambodia. Most American stores don't sell Cambodian foods. Some of the fruits and vegetables that I used to eat just don't grow here. Our climate is very different so we have different foods.

For example, Cambodian people like to cook with a very hot pepper and American stores don't sell it. I got some seeds for this pepper from my cousin, who carried them here from the refugee camp ten years ago.

I learned about gardening when I was in elementary school and high school. Our school had a lot of land. Teams of students would grow gardens on the land. We would do this twice a week, and would have contests to see who could do the best job growing things.

I always loved to grow things, so I planted my own garden here in my yard in America. I grow delicious vegetables, fruits and many kinds of flowers: basil, peppers, Chinese pumpkin, bitter melon, and a long melon that

ខ្ញុំជាអ្នកជាំដំណាំ

is big like watermelon. This melon is so expensive here that you cannot afford to buy it in the grocery store. During the spring and summer, I work in my garden every morning before it gets hot and in the evening just before the sun goes down. In the morning, I weed and I take off the slugs or bugs that are eating the plants. In the evening, I water the garden. If you water the plants mid-day, it might burn the leaves because the sun is shining too hot.

I also grow things inside my house. I grow herbs that I use for medicine and cooking. I dry some of the herbs so that I

can use them during the winter, when they can't grow. Now when I want to cook Cambodian meals, I go to my garden or I use food I have dried from the things I have grown.

I am a cook.

If you visit me, I want you to be comfortable, so I will offer you something to eat. From the time I was young, we always were taught that it would be very rude not to offer guests some food to eat and something to drink.

I like to cook. Food is something like art. It is like painting. If you make vegetables, you want them to taste good. But you also want them to be good looking, nice for your eyes to see, and colorful. You can cut the vegetables in nice shapes. If the food that you eat looks pretty and has nice colors and shapes, then it will taste better to you. You will enjoy eating it more.

I like to experiment with cooking and see what comes out. I cook food that I used to eat in Cambodia. Since I moved to my house here, some of my neighbors have taught me how to make different kinds of meals, and also how to bake cookies, cakes and pies. We like to share food with each other. Whenever one of us cooks something special, we save a little bit for the others to try. After I came to the United States, I also took a class to learn how to make American food. Now I can make Sloppy Joes, apple pie, chili, gingersnaps and lots of other things.

ខ្ញុំជាអ្នកជំស្ល

I am a friend.

I can make friends with anybody. If you are rich or poor, it doesn't make any difference to me. I think that a real friend is someone who always treats you the same—no matter what you have or what happens to you. A real friend is someone who likes you and cares about you.

My friends and I share things with each other. We help each other. We also do things together. My best friend is Tom. He and I share a house together. Tom's great grandparents came to America from Germany many years ago. He explains American ways of doing things and I teach him about Cambodian things. In our house, we each work during the day and we take turns cooking and cleaning.

My brother and my cousins stop by to visit sometime. They moved to Philadelphia from Cambodia three years ago. That made me very happy. Sometimes we all like to go to the park together, or for walks in the woods. I like to go to malls to buy fabric. My friends and I also like to go for rides in inner tubes down the Delaware River. The river and the countryside remind me of home in Cambodia.

ខ្ញុំជាមិត្តម្នាក់

ខ្ញុំជាអ្នកធ្វើសម្លៀកបំពាក់
សំរាប់រាំឬរៀបការ

I am a costume maker.

There are special clothes or costumes that are needed for dances and for Cambodian weddings. I make the traditional clothes that Cambodian people wear for these times.

Some Cambodian people who are getting married hire me to help them. The wedding clothes are very special. They make a bride and groom look like a queen and king. For some parts of the costume, I have to sew thousands of tiny beads into patterns, one at a time. I can't use my sewing machine for this, and it takes me a very long time. I like to do it just right. If something looks wrong, I will take it apart and start again.

I also make all the clothes that I wear for dancing. Some characters must always wear a particular color. Rama, the hero of one long dance story, always must wear green, because the stories say that he was born with greenish skin. His brother, Preah Leak, was born with golden skin according to the stories, so he always wears yellow or golden fabric. The demon characters can wear any color at all— green, red or blue—because they already have masks.

I am a mask maker.

Cambodian dancers sometimes wear masks and crowns. There are crowns for kings and angels. There are masks for terrible ten-faced demons, parrots, and wise men. In Cambodia, people used to tell stories about some of these same characters. When people see the characters appear in a dance, they already know something about the story that the dance is telling.

In Cambodia, mask-makers would make these masks and headpieces which are very important for Cambodian dance. If you don't use them, the dance is not right. Because there was no one to do it for me here in the United States, I had to learn to make masks and crowns for myself. I make them out of papier mâché, mat board, plaster, paint, gold leaf, wire and rhinestones. It takes a long, long time—sometimes three or four weeks—to make just one mask. There are many steps to follow and you have to be very patient.

The mask for the Ramaso character is my favorite one. It has a rooster tail on the top. This is a demon character that I play in a dance called Moni Mekhala.

Moni Mekhala is the name of a female angel. She and Ramaso go to school together, and their teacher gives them a test to see who can fill up a bottle with the most dew. Moni Mekhala lays her scarf on the grass at night, so that in the morning it is covered with lots of dew. Then, she squeezes the dew out into the bottle. Ramaso tries to collect dew drips from every leaf, and it takes him much, much, longer. Moni Mekhala brings the dew to her teacher. Her teacher uses magic to turn the dew into a crystal ball, for a prize. There is much more to this story, and it is great fun to dance. I can tell you that Ramaso finally loses in the end, because he is a bad person, and in this story, the bad person always loses.

25

I am a teacher.

I want to share what I know with other people. I think it is important to teach Cambodian American children some of the traditions from Cambodia that I remember. I also teach children who are not Cambodian if they are interested.

I feel very lucky to know about dance. I know that other people who lived and died long ago helped to create what is now Cambodian court dance. If I don't teach other people, I know that the dance will stop. I don't want that to happen.

I also teach sewing and costume making. Some of the students who learn how to make crowns and medallions are six years old, but they do a good job. You have to start with the simple things first when you are learning anything, and you have to develop your patience because none of this art is done in just an hour!

When I teach, I want people to learn to respect Cambodian history and to understand more about our way of life. I want them to see the beauty in Cambodian dance—the costumes, the feelings and movements of the dance. There is so much to learn.

ខ្ញុំជាគ្រូបង្វាត់

I am a student.

I always like to learn about new things. I am forty years old now, but I think you are never too old to learn. I study English and I try to learn more about life in America.

I am still learning, but it is hard to study Cambodian dance in the United States. There are not many teachers here. Many of the people who knew a lot about the dance died in the war in Cambodia. When I am trying to learn a new dance, I have to find old books and pictures. They are hard to find and the books are not always right. I try to figure out the right way to do different steps and movements. If I have a problem learning something, I sometimes ask my old teachers or other dancers who live here now.

I want to honor the teachers who taught me the dance. If I don't dance correctly, people might think I had poor teachers, and so I am very, very careful.

Some people think I shouldn't dance because I am a man. Other people think that dancing is not serious. Some people call me names because I dance. But in my heart I am a dancer, and I cannot stop.

ខ្ញុំជាទិស្សិត

I am a dancer.

ខ្ញុំជាអ្នករាំ